ALLIGATOR

words by Jack Denton Scott

ALLIGATOR

photographs by Ozzie Sweet

G. P. PUTNAM'S SONS NEW YORK

Published simultaneously in
Canada by General Publishing Co. Limited, Toronto.
Printed in the United States of America
Book design by Kathleen Westray
Library of Congress Cataloging in Publication Data
Scott, Jack Denton
Alligator.
1. Alligators—Juvenile literature.
I. Sweet, Ozzie. II. Title.
QL666.C925S36 1984 597.98 84-9927
ISBN 0-399-21011-3
First impression

Out of the past comes our future.
See you later, alligator—
—JDS

▾▾▾

To my loving wife Diane,
who suggested that we devote a book
to the last great reptile
—OS

▼▼

Alligator or dragon? With its tough, scaly hide, long tail, huge clawed feet and large, fearsome-toothed mouth, this reptile does resemble that mythical monster, the dragon, as it appears in paintings and drawings from centuries past. Only the ability to fly and to breathe fire is missing.

The alligator dates back to the Mesozoic era and lived alongside the extraordinary flying reptiles and the enormous dinosaurs that walked upright on hind feet for 100 million years, dominating life on earth. With crocodiles, they make up the group called crocodilians. Unlike dinosaurs, however, which vanished from the earth 65 million years ago, crocodilians have survived into the twentieth century.

Only two species of alligators remain: the large American alligator *(Alligator mississippiensis),* found in the southeastern United States, and the smaller Chinese alligator *(Alligator sinensis),* which lives in eastern China.

The alligator, North America's largest reptile, got its name from the Spanish *el lagarto ("the lizard").* Early Spanish explorers roaming through Florida sent back to Spain vivid and frightening descriptions of the "terrible giant lizards" they had seen in the New World.

It is likely that the North American alligator got its bad reputation from being confused with the crocodile, which is known to eat people. There are many documented cases around the world of crocodiles stalking and killing humans but comparatively few involving alligators.

crocodiles

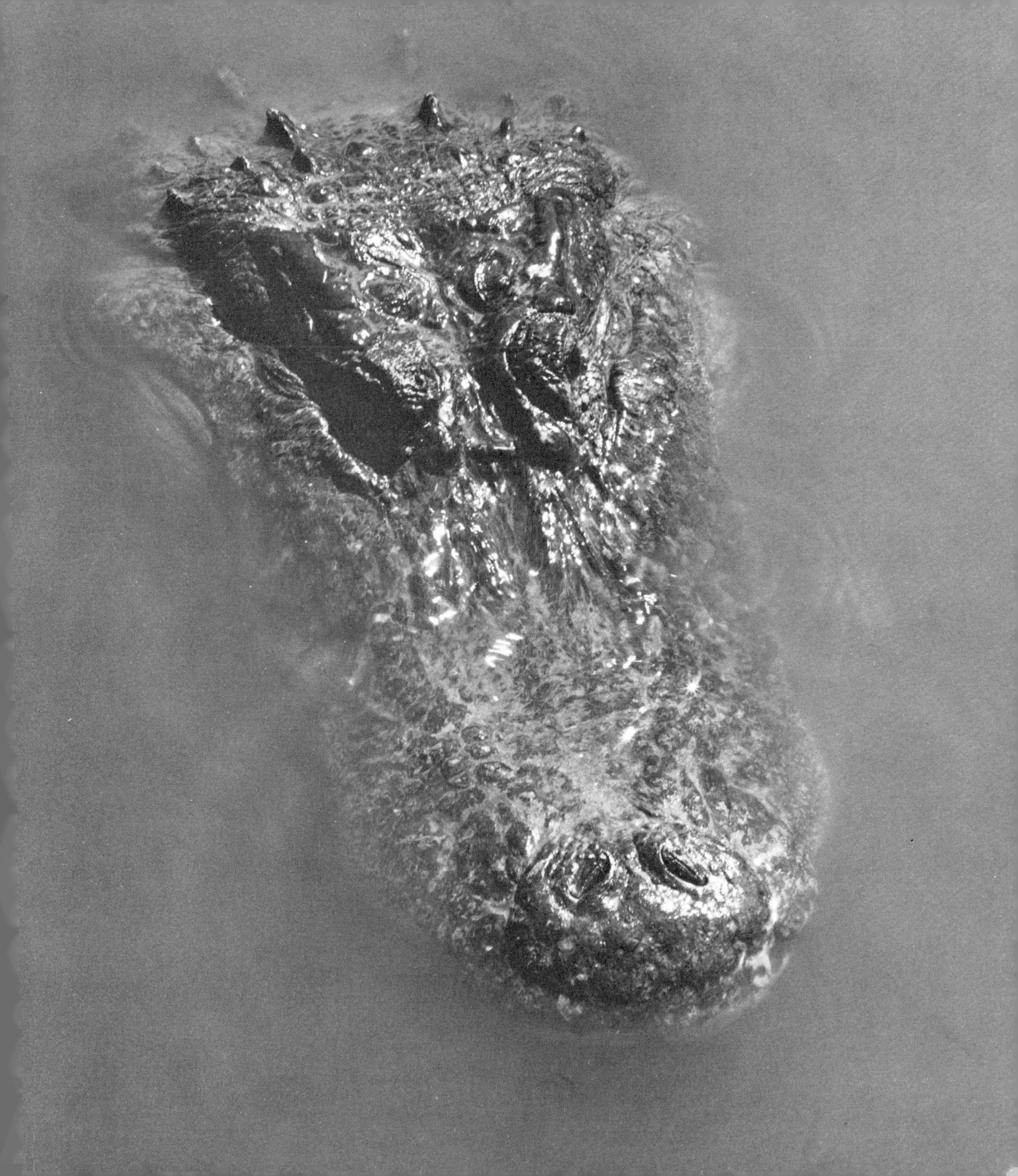

crocodile

Alligators can be easily confused with crocodiles because they so closely resemble one another, but there are specific features that make it easy to tell them apart. The crocodile is slender and more agile, with a long, narrow, pointed snout. The alligator is stockier, with a wide, blunt snout. The alligator's teeth cannot be seen when its jaws are closed; the crocodile's fourth tooth on each side of the lower jaw fits into a niche on the outside of the upper jaw and is clearly visible when the jaws are closed. From this has come the description of a false smile, a "crocodile" smile.

There are fourteen species of crocodiles, many of them dangerous, ranging over tropical areas in Africa, the Pacific Islands, Asia, Australia, South America, Central America, and the U.S. The North American crocodile *(Crocodylus acutus)* lives near salt water and is found in small numbers (probably less than 500) only on the southwest coast of Florida.

Florida has always been the leading alligator state, with such a conspicuous population that some state maps refer to one state highway as Alligator Alley. Highway 538, at Andytown, north of Miami, is the junction where a two-and-a-half-hour drive begins through the wilderness of the Big Cypress Swamp west to the Everglades and on to Naples. This is prime alligator country.

Originally, alligators were found as far north as the Carolinas and west to the Rio Grande. In the late 1700s, an explorer wrote that the reptiles were so numerous in the St. Johns River in northeastern Florida that he could have crossed the river by walking on their backs.

alligator

That large population did not last long: When it was discovered that its serrated, leathery, shiny hide—especially the belly skin—made such handsome and durable billfolds, belts, handbags, purses, and luggage that people were willing to pay high prices to own them, the alligator was in trouble.

At the height of the hide trade, hunters were getting $20 a foot for the skins, with a bonus for the younger alligators, whose hides and bellies were smoother and more resilient. Manufacturers estimated that most leather was worth about $2 a foot, but alligator skin was worth $15 an inch! A high-quality leather bag was sold in stores for $200; an alligator bag retailed at an astounding $2,000.

For over a century, alligators were hunted relentlessly. In the nineteenth century, 3 million were killed in Florida alone. In Louisiana, 2 million were killed between 1865 and 1957.

In 1946, outdoor editor Dave Newell reported, "On a recent trip to the Everglades and the Ten Thousand Islands during which we spent two weeks in some of the wildest and most inaccessible areas in Florida, we saw only *one* small alligator. Twenty years ago we would have seen five hundred in the same length of time."

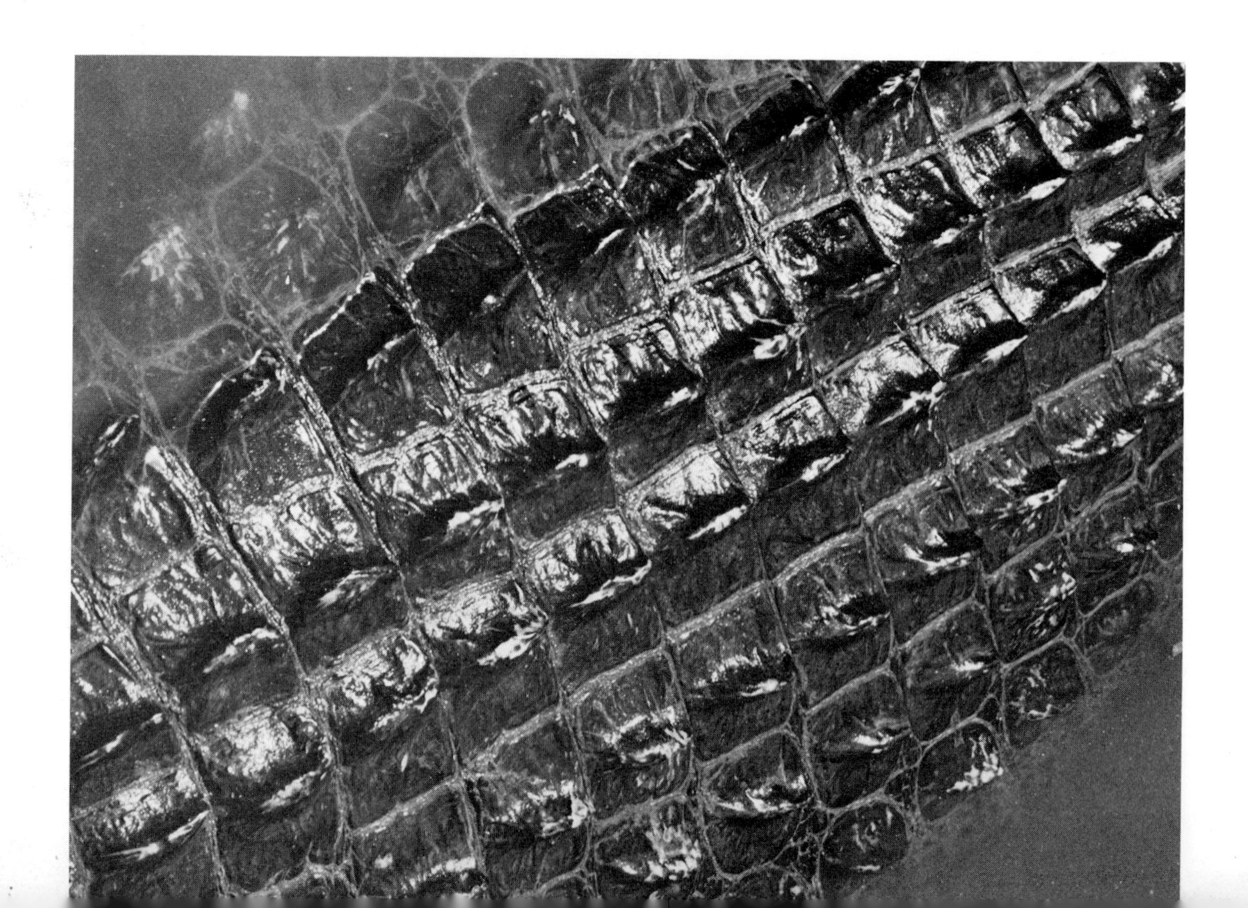

Similar reports continued to appear from all over the Southeast, where the alligator had lived peaceably and prolifically for centuries. There were no laws regulating or preventing shipment of alligator skins interstate, and foreign buyers came from all over the world to take advantage of what had become an open market.

By 1961, the alligator population had dwindled so alarmingly that Florida was forced to move to eliminate the hunting season, which in some areas permitted the killing of alligators 6 feet or more in length. But the profit was so tempting that poachers ignored the law and continued taking all ages and sizes of the reptiles, even stealing them from alligator farms that had been created for the tourist trade and for research.

The slaughter continued in all of the alligator states for another eight years until conservationists, naturalists, biologists, and various officials of the southeastern states convinced Congress that this was a wildlife crisis equal to the one that had made the buffalo extinct. Finally, Congress passed the Endangered Species Act (1969), banning shipment of alligators or their hides across state lines. Eventually the Endangered Species Act was broadened to include the crocodile, the grizzly bear, the gray wolf, the eagle and many more waning species of wild creatures, totalling 110. The alligator and the crocodile however, were the most ancient of the species, and despite the help from Congress, were fast-disappearing.

In 1972, Florida finally passed laws that levied fines of $5,000 and five years in prison for persons capturing or killing any size alligator. Similar laws in other states eventually brought the killing to a halt.

Since then, the alligator has made an amazing comeback, a testament to its talent for survival. In less than twenty years, it again populates Florida and Louisiana, and is found all the way up to the coast of North Carolina, as well as ranging west through the cypress swamps and blackwater rivers of the Gulf States to the marshes of Arkansas and Texas. Wildlife biologists believe that the astounding recovery already totals over 1 million in states where alligators were never overabundant, and in excess of 1 million in Florida alone, followed by about ½ million in Louisiana.

Florida's 6 million acres of lakes and wetlands have always been superb alligator country, along with the vast Everglades, which gives the alligator the water and seclusion it must have.

The North American alligator is one of approximately 6,000 species and four orders of reptiles remaining on the planet. Sixteen orders thrived during the Age of Reptiles by which the Mesozoic era is sometimes known; the other 12 orders vanished 63 million years ago. Since that time, snakes probably have changed the most, alligators the least.

It seems the alligator was so ideally created for survival that there were no natural reasons for change. Longer legs might have allowed it to move more quickly on land, but land is not the alligator's true element anyway. It is semiaquatic and—for short distances at least—can run as fast as a person.

In water, the alligator is so fast that it can catch a fish easily. Its long tail, moving from side to side, acts as a powerful paddle, propelling the big reptile through water almost as rapidly as a motorized craft. In fact, hunters in outboard motorboats have difficulty keeping up with swimming alligators.

Amazingly, the alligator can even regrow the lost tip of its valuable tail. For many years it was thought that the alligator used its tail as a weapon for flailing at enemies and stunning and downing prey, and there are old accounts of alligators using their long tails to sweep humans into the water, where they were devoured. None of this is fact: The mouth is the alligator's only seizing and defensive mechanism. One biologist, watching out for the tail in an effort to verify reports of its deadliness, almost had his leg broken by an alligator's tied but still powerful snout!

The alligator's skin, or hide, is among its most important assets for survival. (Ironically, the same feature almost led to its destruction as a species.) The thick, tough hide—sheathed with scales containing scutes, or hard circles of bone—forms a protective waterproof dorsal plating almost as strong as metal. This makes the alligator as nearly invulnerable as a submarine as it glides through the water.

Also like a submarine, the alligator has a "periscope" (elevated eyes) and a "snorkel" breathing tube (nostrils). With these important protuberant features, it can see above water and breathe while the rest of its body is submerged.

Thus, almost invisible, it can drift or swim slowly toward prey, barely disturbing the surface of the water, until it lunges with amazing speed and grabs the target with jaws so powerful that they clamp the victim in a viselike grip. Forty teeth in each jaw, graduated in size, make it impossible for even the smallest of prey to escape. Those teeth even have backups, replacement teeth that grow in as older ones are lost. This does not occur during the entire life span, however: Thirty-year-old alligators have been found that were virtually toothless.

Its teeth, combined with power, speed, and "invisibility," make the alligator a formidable predator. One observer saw a Florida alligator come out of a lake in a blur of motion, snatch a marsh rabbit standing on shore, then disappear into the water. He described it as a bad-dream sequence, occurring so fast that it seemed like a hallucination.

The alligator has a submarinelike system of fleshy valves that automatically close when it is diving, protecting nostrils, ears, and throat from water. A third, transparent eyelid enables it to see without getting water in its eyes. Imbedded in its eyes are thousands of tiny crystals that collect all available light, giving the alligator keen sight underwater, even at night. It can actually remain underwater for over an hour.

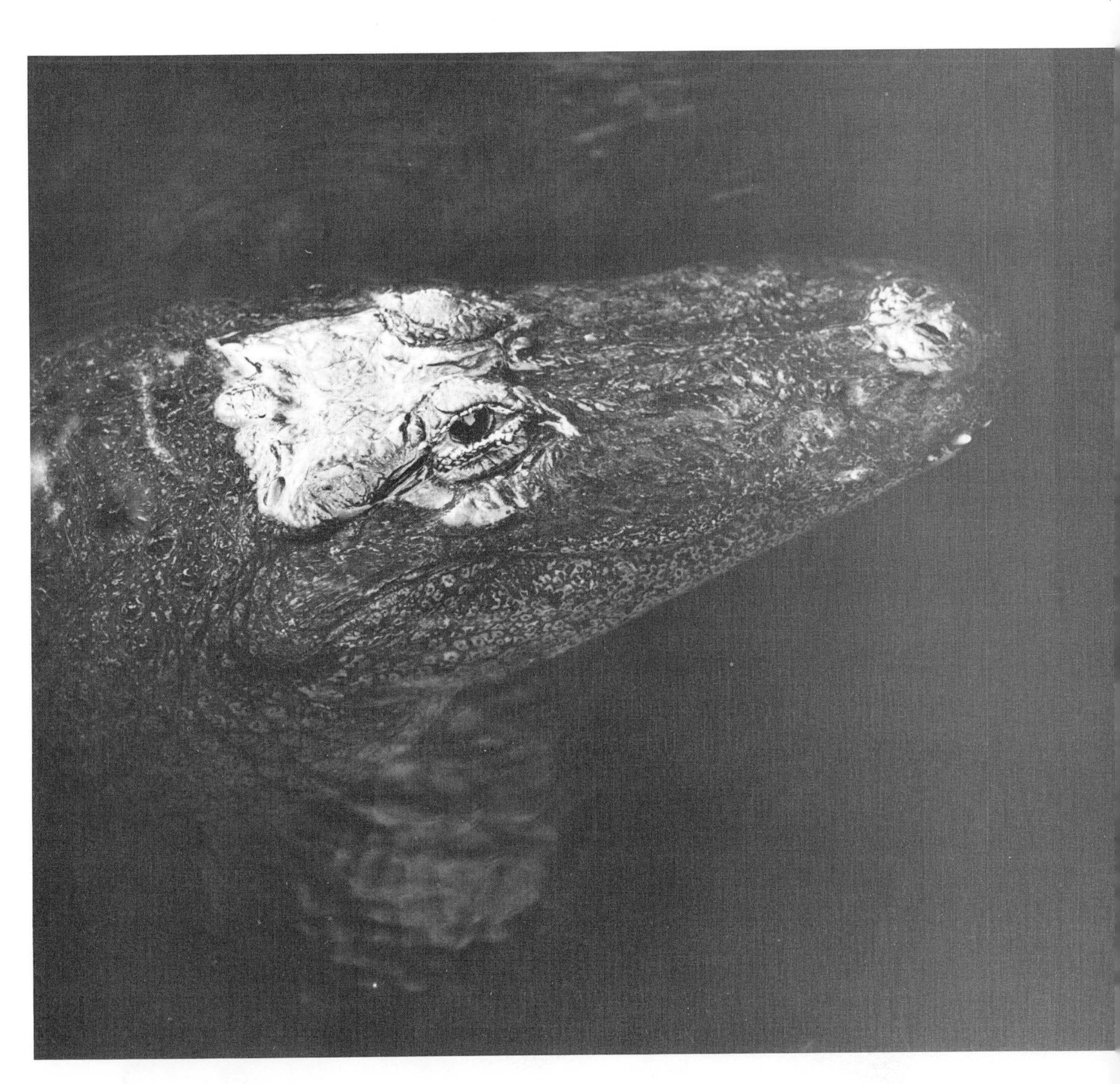

Alligators can go for as long as four months without food. In the northernmost southern states, because of the colder weather there, alligators sometimes go into a state of semihibernation for a period lasting that long. The alligator's most common food is live natural prey that inhabits water or marshlands and may include fish, frogs, mink, muskrats, marsh rabbits, rats, snakes, turtles, and waterfowl. It also eats any carrion it may find. But the alligator is selective too. It quickly snatches and immediately eats nonvenomous snakes, but it is cautious with venomous varieties, first biting

them to kill them, then carefully tossing them around before swallowing them. The alligator does not chew food but swallows it whole, tearing and crushing prey into manageable mouthfuls. Captive alligators, fed pieces of beef and chicken, refused the food when it was mixed with canned cat food.

Although alligators prefer a warm climate, they can tolerate the colder weather of some southern states such as North Carolina. When ponds freeze, alligators solve breathing problems by smashing holes in the ice, then pushing their snouts through.

Normally, any water shortages they encounter are readily brought under their control, since in many instances alligators construct and maintain their own waterholes or ponds. During times of drought, the so-called 'gator hole may even be the only source of water for other wildlife in the area.

In marshland, both the male and female use their tails and mouths to excavate grass and mud. They dig down until they reach water, sometimes creating a pond as much as 25 feet wide. When that is completed, a tunnel is dug, often running 20 feet from the pond, with an area wide enough at the end where the alligator can turn around and exit head first. This small den extends above the water level, so oxygen is available while it is resting or sleeping.

The pond created by the alligator is carefully maintained—deepened, widened, weeds cleared, as needed. Not only is the waterhole used as a refuge for the adult alligator that dug it, with its escape hatch for fleeing from its only enemy, man, but if the hole is excavated by a female it is used by her offspring as their only haven from their many enemies. Biologists have observed three consecutive age groups of alligators near an active hole.

Biologists who study the alligator continue to marvel at the remarkable physical attributes the primitive creature has to compensate for its small brain. Not as clever as the fox or the raccoon, the alligator is an amazing survivor in its own right. Some scientists even believe that young alligators are aided in their inexperienced food-searching efforts with a kind of radar, tiny sensitive organs evenly spaced on each side of the snout, which they use more often than eyesight to locate food.

The alligator has an exceptional homing sense, unerringly returning to home territory after forcibly being relocated. One biologist tracked a radio-tagged, 11-foot relocated male that waddled 35 miles across land, crossing cornfields and a major highway on the way from its new home to the pond where it had grown up.

It also has been established that the alligator can survive wounds that would be fatal to other animals. A South Carolina biologist found an alligator whose upper jaw had been ripped off. He took it home where it lived without problems, except for an occasional sunburned tongue. Florida biologist Denis David says it is not uncommon to find two- or three-legged alligators that appear to live normally, and he has seen several humpbacked animals that have obviously had their backs broken and survived.

But perhaps foremost among all the attributes that have kept alligators with us longer than almost any other wild creature is their remarkable reproductive process, their constant, timeless reestablishment of their unique species.

There are many misconceptions about that reproductive process. Some accounts claim that only the male bellows, or roars, signaling that he is looking for a mate. In fact, both the male and female bellow, and not just during the mating season, but whenever they are inclined to do so.

That roar is extraordinary in itself, coming from a creature that is soundless, except for an occasional grunt or hiss. It is projected by the alligator inhaling an excessive amount of oxygen, then abruptly exhaling it. Among the eeriest sounds of the Everglades are those roars one hears as dusk settles over that vast, mysterious, swampy area—primeval sounds that turn the clock back to another age.

No biologist has yet discovered how alligators find one another when it is time to mate. They do know that it is always in the spring, usually April, when the motivation to reproduce the species occurs. Some of the experts believe that the females emit a peculiar and penetrating musk from a gland, a scent that attracts males, much like that of a female dog in heat, but this has never been verified. The scent is not evident to humans.

It seems that both sexes begin searching for mates almost simultaneously. This does not happen, however, until both reptiles are at least 6 feet long, at which time they are between six and ten years of age and sexually mature. Both males and females search aggressively, but once a pair find each other, it is only the male who remains aggressive. He follows the female wherever she goes. Males have been observed scurrying after females on land and water for as long as two weeks, until the female apparently decides that the situation is right and that the anxious male pursuing her is the right alligator.

Another misconception: It would seem logical that when two dragonlike, ferocious-looking creatures mate there should be loud roars and a lashing of their prehensile tails. Surprisingly, alligators are graceful and gentle in their courtship and in the actual breeding.

There have been vivid descriptions of males fighting bloody battles over females, but fights are rare. Biologists have seen them happen, however, where there are large populations of alligators and not enough females.

Much of the courtship occurs in water, with the two cavorting like porpoises, the male swimming after the female in a game of tag that can continue for three days, even sometimes as long as seventeen. If man disturbs their mating activities, often the pair will simply stop and not mate until the following spring.

Biologists who have seen and photographed the mating claim that it is astonishing to see these huge, prehistoric creatures lying side by side in shallow water as playful as puppies. The male will carefully reach a scaly forelimb out of the water and gently stroke the female. She can almost be heard purring, observers report. The male then lightly butts her throat and rubs against it, at the same time blowing bursts of bubbles past her cheeks.

This is repeated several times before the actual mating takes place in the water, the female finally raising her tail and bending it away from the male. The union itself usually is completed in less than five minutes. The male then abruptly leaves the female and returns to his own territory. He does not mate with another, nor does the female. For both, the breeding session is over.

Approximately two months after the pair have parted, the female goes to her own pond, or near other water. This seems to be necessary for the successful incubation of her eggs. Once she has found a safe location—always in a shady, isolated place where there is dense vegetation—this great reptile takes on some of the characteristics of a bird. She constructs her nest close to the water, but elevated so it cannot be flooded. She works at night, probably because she is less likely to be observed then.

The fact that female alligators prepare nests to receive their eggs has contributed to some scientists' belief that reptiles evolved from birds, or were a combination of bird and reptile. They point to evidence of the flying reptiles of the Upper Jurassic period, one example of which was discovered in Germany. This specimen was called Archaeopteryx ("ancient wing"). About the size of a crow, it had a long neck, a long reptilian tail, and a reptilian head—and feathers. There also were large flying reptiles called Phytosaurs that looked like alligators.

Using a curious lateral movement of body and tail, she skillfully scrapes mud, leaves, and other vegetation into a conical heap about 5 feet wide and 3 feet high. While she is building the nest, she continually crawls over the sides and top, packing it down. The nest is completed in about three days. With a hind foot, she then carefully scoops out a deepish cavity in the center. About four hours after this, she perches on top like some great weird bird and arranges her vent over the nest cavity, placing her hind feet in such a way as to cushion the fall of the eggs as they emerge. She lays an average of thirty, 3-inch-long white eggs, but often as many as fifty. Observers say that despite her size and ungainly movements and appearance, the female alligator completes all these tasks with grace and dexterity.

Much colorful information has circulated regarding the approximately three-month period before and after the hatching of the eggs. A good deal of it is untrue, however. For instance, it has been said that the female keeps the nest moist with her urine, or carries water in her mouth and sprays it on the nest; that she guards the nest night and day, and will fight to the death to protect it; that when the young are hatching they grunt and their mother rushes to the nest and uncovers it so they can easily emerge; that she either guides them to the water or picks the laggards up and carries them there in her mouth.

According to Wilfred T. Neill, a former professor of zoology and an expert who has observed captive and wild alligators for years, the female does keep the nest moist with water, but water that comes from her dripping body after she has swum in the nearby pond or lagoon. She does guard the nest, never straying more than a few yards from it, except when she is foraging for food; and she probably will kill smaller creatures bent on raiding the nest for the

eggs, but with man she is mostly hiss and bluff. Professor Neill has often disturbed and approached alligators at their nests and been threatened, but never attacked. In fact, on several occasions the female has retreated when he persisted in his advances on the nest.

When she is not cooling off in the water or looking for food, the female alligator often rests with her throat pressed against the nest. Some scientists think this may be to provide her with a sort of "thermometer" by which to judge when the nest requires heat or moisture.

When the young are ready to break out of the eggs (usually late July, after a late April mating), they slit the egg shell open with a "caruncle," a tiny, hard pointed growth on the end of their snouts. When they emerge, still buried in the nest, they do grunt or yelp, but the female seldom rushes to uncover them. They usually make their own way out of the moist, warm "incubator" of grass, leaves, and vegetation, just as hatching turtles wiggle upward out of the sunwarmed sand where the mother turtle has buried her eggs.

Once they squirm up out of the nest, the newborn alligators instinctively make their way to the nearest water, both for safety and food. The female does not lead them there. In fact, though a female has been known to watch after her offspring for a few weeks (or for as long as they remain with her), and sometimes protects them from their enemies, this is rare. She, like most reptiles, leaves her offspring once they are hatched. More often, the entire brood of baby alligators often disperses when they reach water, abandoning the female almost immediately.

The $8\frac{1}{2}$-inch yellow-and-black hatchlings do not have to search for food for the first few days. Their stomachs are distended with the unabsorbed yolk from the egg that furnishes their nourishment. After it has been absorbed, they begin their never-ending hunt for food—insects, fish, frogs, anything small enough for them to catch and handle, if they aren't caught first themselves. For the young alligator's enemies are many: wading water birds, mink, otters, raccoons, snakes, and man.

Fortunately, young alligators are relatively safe from humans today, due to stringent laws. But before that, baby alligators were caught, peddled to souvenir and pet shops, and sold to tourists by the thousands. Buyers were often dismayed later when they found that their little pets did not stay small: The alligators that survive these early months grow about 12 inches a year for the first five years. When these baby alligators began to snap at the hands that fed them, they were hurriedly released into lakes, ponds, and rivers, usually far from their homeland in the southeastern U.S. Countless numbers died of exposure in freezing weather, or were killed by alarmed people who found them.

Those hunters who caught baby alligators were lucky if they were not attacked by adult alligators. For alligators are remarkable among reptiles in that any adult hearing the yelping distress call of a young one will rush to defend it. The adults are also patient with young alligators, not only protecting them whenever they can, but permitting them to wander through their exclusive territories without molesting them. Sometimes these half-grown alligators travel in groups, but when they have attained the length of 4 feet, they apparently are no longer considered adolescents and are driven out of areas occupied by adults. They then must travel individually overland to try to find a swamp, marsh, or pond where they can take up residence.

Although adult alligators establish their own territories, they often gather on the banks of rivers, lakes, or ponds or any area of water. In Florida, in just one 5-mile area where springs had created collections of excess water, seventy-five alligators were counted. This is called a "spring-run." The Everglades used to be prime alligator territory, but today in Florida, lakes attract the largest populations. Orange Lake, in the north-central section of the state, has 6,000 alligators occupying its 9,000 acres; Georgia's Okefenokee National Wildlife Refuge has 100 alligators per mile; and Lake Seminole in southwestern Georgia has "too many to count." So, in some areas, alligators comprise a society whether they seek it or not.

They mainly get along well together, although as with all wild creatures, fights over territory sometimes take place. Adult males are zealous in guarding and defending their territories, and if another male persists in trying to trespass there could be a battle.

Usually, however, the resident of the territory can bluff the other into moving on without fighting. Biologists who have seen males battle say it is a fierce and sometimes bloody action, as they are so large and strong and well equipped by nature to defend themselves.

There is also an alligator pecking order dictated by size. The largest alligator dominates the group, and the others make way for him, even giving up a favorite lounging place on a bank or shore if the dominant alligator wants to occupy it. The females rarely grow beyond 9 feet, but many males attain a length of 13 feet and more. The longest on record was a rare 19 feet, 2 inches; the heaviest weighed over 1,000 pounds.

Biologists have speculated, by studying captive and wild alligators, that they grow rapidly for the first eight years, more slowly until the sixteenth year, then continue to grow, but almost imperceptibly, for another ten years. At that point a maximum growth has been reached. Typically, growth slows somewhat once a length of 6 feet is attained, especially in the case of females.

It is a fallacy that alligators live to be one hundred years or even older. They do not live as long as man, and are fortunate if they reach fifty. And studies of captive alligators conclude that females may not live much beyond thirty.

Today's alligators face two new survival problems: As more and more southern wetlands are being drained for human habitation, the alligators' range is shrinking. And they are considered by many people, especially Northerners who have never seen a live alligator, as menaces. In Florida alone, there are about 4,000 complaints a year, with 2,000 "nuisance" alligators relocated annually. Problem alligators, those who have actually attacked people seemingly without provocation, are killed.

Are alligators dangerous? Yes. And no. Biologists report that normally, unless cornered or provoked, they will usually retreat from people. We have overrun much of their territory, changing or even occupying their natural habitat. If in self-protection a confused alligator takes over a pond on a new golf course, or near recently completed residences, it should not be teased or fed, but removed by persons trained for that purpose.

When alligators are relocated, they are usually taken to areas where there are few of them and little civilization. Several years ago, 2,000 surplus alligators from Lousisana were transplanted successfully to Arkansas and Mississippi after landowners and timber companies in those states had asked for the reptiles to help control an overpopulation of beavers that were harming forest lands.

Like most wild animals (bears in state parks, for example), alligators that have lost their fear of man through constant exposure to them can also be dangerous. Coaxing them to come closer for a photograph or tempting them with food could be asking for trouble. Usually, alligators, almost in a reflex motion, immediately snap at whatever startles or threatens them.

Alligators in water are fascinating to watch. As they surface and dive, race after one another, lie resting, move through growths of pond lilies, make a surprise appearance amid algae, or coast along the surface with their fearsome-looking heads jutting out from the water, it is clear that they are masters of their watery domain. No one should contest that, or try to share the water with them. In one tragic incident, a young girl took a swim while canoeing on Florida's Myakka River, and was killed by an 11-foot alligator. Wildlife authorities who investigated said that the Myakka River ran near a popular state park where thousands of visitors hand-fed the alligators. Because they were very familiar with people, the alligators had no fear of them and had come to associate them with food.

With 99 percent of the fresh water in Florida suitable habitat for alligators, and with thousands of people using those waters for recreational purposes, the state's wildlife experts consider it remarkable that on the average only five attacks are reported yearly. Only three deaths from alligator attacks have been documented since the Florida Wildlife Department began keeping records in the late 1950s.

Although beavers, foxes, raccoons, and other fairly large mammals are the alligators' natural prey, there are frequent reports of alligators stalking and killing dogs. A dog off its leash and running unaccompanied in alligator territory is always in danger. The big reptiles have no way of knowing that they are not fair game.

After its near extinction, the alligator is doing so well today—averaging an increase of about 25 percent every two years in most of its range—that protective regulations are being relaxed somewhat. It is still classified as endangered in Alabama, North Carolina, inland South Carolina, Mississippi, and inland Texas. However, in the coastal regions of Georgia, South Carolina, and Texas, and throughout Florida, alligators are now federally labeled as merely "threatened," which means that the way is being cleared for restricted hunting. In Louisiana, they are classified in bureaucratic language as "threatened by similarity of appearance," which means some hunting is permitted. That term was adopted to prevent poachers from killing alligators considered "endangered" in, say, Alabama, then slipping their skins into a collection of legal hides from Louisiana, where the alligator population is now abundant.

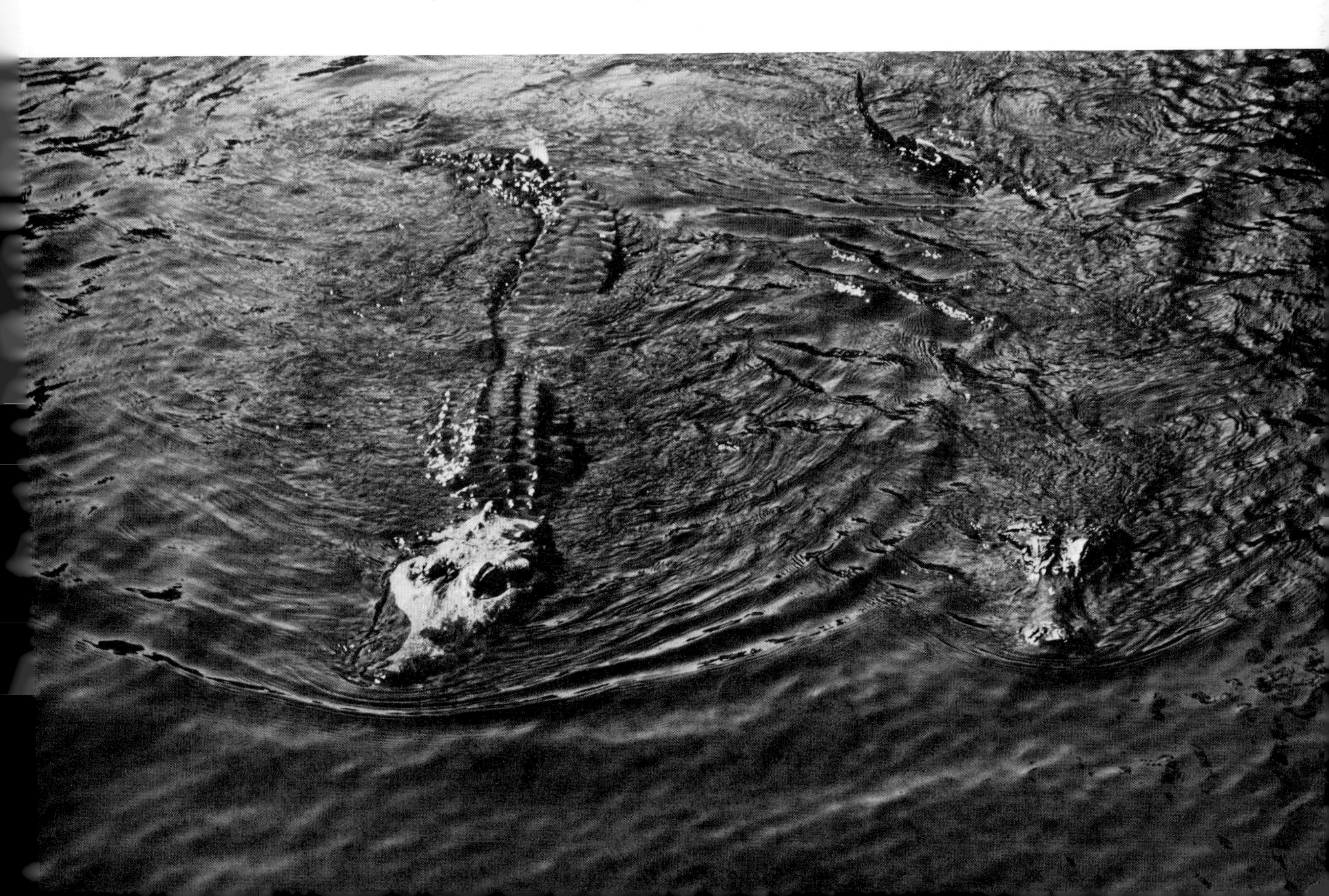

Louisiana, the first state to make hunting legal again in 1981, limits it to one month in all counties and speculates that the yearly harvest could total as many as 20,000 alligators from the state population of 450,000. Limits are strict: One 4-foot (or larger) alligator is allowed a hunter for each 100 acres, and the hunter must either own the land or have the owner deed him the right to take the legal limit. Texas is negotiating for a similar arrangement.

Florida, which almost considers the alligator its state animal, has no open season. It is trying an experimental, three-week, state-directed hunt, with 20 hunters selected by lottery, hunting just three lakes, and with only 300 alligators to be taken. This hunt is being studied by biologists to determine if a legal hunting season is logical for the future.

Although hunters, and some officials, in certain southern states are clamoring for an open season, supervisory federal and state wildlife authorities are proceeding with caution. Hide dealers are still waiting in the wings with money. In 1981, Florida sold over 700 hides at $22 a foot.

State-regulated alligator farms are thriving in Florida and Louisiana, based on the belief that the reptiles are a renewable resource that can be raised in captivity both for profit and for the benefit of the species. Some wildlife specialists agree, and are convinced that the farms will not only relieve pressure from hunters, but that wildlife management can control, and even direct, future alligator populations for the reptiles' benefit.

Presently, alligator farms, hunters, and wildlife personnel (in Florida, officials rely on the so-called nuisance reptiles) are supplying hides to the trade, and again alligator "leather" is being used in various nationally advertised products, such as belts, watchbands, and wallets.

And now there is a new product interest: alligator meat as a food. It is becoming so popular in the South that in the last annual tally in Florida, the sale of alligator meat actually netted more than the hides: Hides went for $26,009, meat for $40,000. In that state, trimmed, quality cuts are currently selling for as much as $5 a pound. State-inspected, and sold only to restaurants, the tail meat (preferred) is white, and the body meat red, not unlike beef in appearance. The taste is said to be mild, with a slight seafood flavor. And Louisiana has recently inaugurated an annual "Festival of Alligator Cuisine" based on the theme that the meat is nutritious, has little fat, and can be used in as many appetizing ways as more conventional meats.

Conservationists and wildlife authorities who have fought to bring the alligator back from extinction are watching this unexpected and somewhat macabre development with shocked attention. They claim, however, that even if the idea of eating alligator catches on, and is not just a passing food fad, today's alligator farms are so successful and wildlife supervision so alert and strict that it seems unlikely the alligator will ever again be pushed to the brink of extinction.

Furthermore, public interest in and understanding of our oldest wildlife resident is growing. This, coupled with wildlife experts widely circulating facts versus myths, is producing heartening evidence that America's alligator is finally being appreciated for what it is—one of our most valuable and unusual natural treasures.

INDEX